Edgar Allan Poe, Carl Theodor Eben

Vier amerikanische Gedichte

Edgar Allan Poe, Carl Theodor Eben

Vier amerikanische Gedichte

ISBN/EAN: 9783743434769

Hergestellt in Europa, USA, Kanada, Australien, Japan

Cover: Foto ©Andreas Hilbeck / pixelio.de

Manufactured and distributed by brebook publishing software (www.brebook.com)

Edgar Allan Poe, Carl Theodor Eben

Vier amerikanische Gedichte

FOUR AMERICAN POEMS.

THE RAVEN. By Edgar Allan Poe.
THE BELLS. By the same.
LENORE. By the same.
THE ROSE. By James Russell Lowell.

Metrically translated into German

BY

CHARLES THEODORE EBEN.

PHILADELPHIA:
FREDERICK LEYPOLDT.
1864.

Vier amerikanische Gedichte.

Der Rabe. Von Edgar Allan Poe.
Die Glocken. Von demselben.
Lenore. Von demselben.
Die Rose. Von James Russell Lowell.

Metrisch in's Deutsche übersetzt
von
Carl Theodor Eben.

Philadelphia:
Friedrich Leypoldt.
1864.

THESE TRANSLATIONS

ARE RESPECTFULLY INSCRIBED

TO

William E. Whitman, Esq.,

OF PHILADELPHIA,

THROUGH WHOSE GENEROUS ENCOURAGEMENT THEY
ARE GIVEN TO THE PUBLIC.

TO THE READER.

The following poems of E. A. Poe and J. R. Lowell are herewith offered to the Public in metrical German versions, taken from a collection of translations comprising specimens from every American poet of reputation, from the earliest dawn of American Literature up to the present day, in chronological order, and accompanied by biographical sketches and a concise critical review of the poetical literature of America. Should the meed of an encouraging reception be awarded to the present labor of the Undersigned, the publication of the larger work will be hastened with all the speed that circumstances admit of.

Philadelphia, November 1863.

EBEN.

An den Leser.

Die nachfolgenden Gedichte von E. A. Poe und J. R. Lowell werden hiermit dem Publikum in metrischer deutscher Uebertragung geboten. Dieselben sind einer Sammlung von Ueberſetzungen entnommen, die ſämmtliche amerikaniſchen Dichter von Ruf, von der erſten Dämmerung der amerikaniſchen Literatur bis auf den heutigen Tag, in chronologiſcher Ordnung, von biographiſchen Skizzen und einer literar-hiſtoriſchen Einleitung begleitet, umfaſſen wird. Sollte den vorliegenden Proben eine ermuthigende Aufnahme zu Theil werden, ſo wird die Herausgabe des größeren Werkes ſo raſch erfolgen, als die Umſtände es geſtatten.

Eben.

Philadelphia im November 1863.

The Raven.

Once upon a midnight dreary,
  While I pondered, weak and weary,
Over many a quaint and curious
    Volume of forgotten lore—
While I nodded, nearly napping,
Suddenly there came a tapping,
As of some one gently rapping,
    Rapping at my chamber door;
" 'Tis some visiter," I muttered,
    "Tapping at my chamber door—
      Only this and nothing more."

Der Rabe.

Mitternacht umgab mich schaurig,
Als ich einsam, trüb und traurig,
Sinnend saß und las von mancher
Längst verklung'nen Mähr' und Lehr' —
Als ich schon mit matten Blicken
Im Begriff, in Schlaf zu nicken,
Hörte plötzlich ich ein Ticken
An die Zimmerthüre her;
„Ein Besuch wohl noch," so dacht' ich,
„Den der Zufall führet her —
Ein Besuch und sonst Nichts mehr."

Ah, distinctly I remember,
It was in the bleak December,
And each separate dying ember
    Wrought its ghost upon the floor.
Eagerly I wished the morrow;—
Vainly I had sought to borrow
From my books surcease of sorrow—
    Sorrow for the lost Lenore—
For the rare and radiant maiden
    Whom the angels name Lenore—
    Nameless here for evermore!

And the silken sad uncertain
Rustling of each purple curtain
Thrilled me—filled me with fantastic
    Terrors never felt before;
So that now, to still the beating
Of my heart, I stood repeating,
" 'Tis some visiter entreating
    Entrance at my chamber door—
Some late visiter entreating
    Entrance at my chamber door;
    This it is and nothing more."

Der Rabe.

Wohl hab' ich's im Sinn behalten,
Im December war's, im kalten,
Und gespenstige Gestalten
    Warf des Feuers Schein umher.
Sehnlich wünscht' ich mir den Morgen,
Keine Lind'rung war zu borgen
Aus den Büchern für die Sorgen —
    Für die Sorgen, tief und schwer,
Um die Sel'ge, die Lenoren
    Nennt der Engel heilig Heer —
        Hier, ach, nennt sie Niemand mehr!

Jedes Rauschen der Gardinen,
Die mir wie Gespenster schienen,
Füllte mich mit bangen Schrecken —
    Schrecken, nie gefühlt vorher;
So daß, um mein Herz, das zagte,
Zu beruhigen, ich sagte:
„Ein Besuch wohl noch, der's wagte,
    In der Nacht zu kommen her —
Ein Besuch, der sich verspätet
    Und zu mir nun eilet her;
        Dies allein und sonst Nichts mehr."

Presently my soul grew stronger;
Hesitating then no longer,
"Sir," said I, "or Madam, truly
    Your forgiveness I implore
But the fact is, I was napping,
And so gently you came rapping,
And so faintly you came tapping,
    Tapping at my chamber door,
That I scarce was sure I heard you"—
    Here I opened wide the door:—
        Darkness there and nothing more.

Deep into that darkness peering,
Long I stood there wondering, fearing,
Doubting, dreaming dreams no mortals
    Ever dared to dream before;
But the silence was unbroken,
And the stillness gave no token,
And the only word there spoken
    Was the whispered word, "Lenore?"
This I whispered, and an echo
    Murmured back the word, "Lenore!"—
        Merely this and nothing more.

Neugestärkt nach diesen Worten,
Oeffnete ich stracks die Pforten:
„Dame oder Herr," so sprach ich,
 „Bitte um Verzeihung sehr!
Doch ich war mit matten Blicken
Im Begriff, in Schlaf zu nicken,
Und so leis scholl Euer Ticken
 An die Zimmerthüre her,
Daß ich kaum es recht vernommen;
 Doch nun seid willkommen sehr!" —
  Dunkel da und sonst Nichts mehr.

Düster in das Dunkel schauend,
Stand ich lange starr und grauend,
Träume träumend, die hienieden
 Nie ein Mensch geträumt vorher;
Zweifel schwarz den Sinn bethöret,
Nichts die Stille draußen störet,
Nur das Eine Wort man höret,
 Nur „Lenore?" tönt es her;
Selbst rief ich es, und „Lenore!"
 Trug das Echo trauernd her —
  Dies allein und sonst Nichts mehr.

Back into the chamber turning,
All my soul within me burning,
Soon again I heard a tapping,
    Something louder than before.
"Surely," said I, "surely that is
Something at my window lattice:
Let me see, then, what thereat is,
    And this mystery explore—
Let my heart be still a moment
    And this mystery explore;—
        'Tis the wind and nothing more."

Open here I flung the shutter,
When, with many a flirt and flutter,
In there stepped a stately Raven
    Of the saintly days of yore.
Not the least obeisance made he;
Not a minute stopped or stayed he;
But with mien of lord or lady,
    Perched above my chamber door—
Perched upon a bust of Pallas
    Just above my chamber door—
        Perched, and sat, and nothing more.

Der Rabe.

Als ich nun mit tiefem Bangen
Wieder in's Gemach gegangen,
Hört' ich bald ein neues Pochen,
    Etwas lauter als vorher.
„Sicher," sprach ich da mit Beben,
„An das Fenster pocht es eben;
Nun, wohlan, so laß mich streben,
    Daß ich mir das Ding erklär' —
Still, mein Herz, daß ich mit Ruhe
    Dies Geheimniß mir erklär' —
      Wohl der Wind und sonst Nichts mehr."

Riß das Fenster auf jetzunder,
Und herein stolzirt — o Wunder!
Ein gewalt'ger, hochbejahrter
    Rabe schwirrend zu mir her.
Keinen Gruß, kein Dankeszeichen
Würdigte er mir zu reichen,
Stolz und stattlich, sonder Gleichen,
    Flog nach meiner Thüre er —
Flog nach einer Pallasbüste
    Ob der Thüre hoch und hehr —
      Setzte sich und sonst Nichts mehr.

Then this ebony bird beguiling
My sad fancy into smiling,
By the grave and stern decorum
Of the countenance it wore,
"Though thy crest be shorn and shaven,
Thou", I said, "art sure no craven,
Ghastly grim and ancient Raven
Wandering from the Nightly shore—
Tell me what thy lordly name is
On the Night's Plutonian shore!"
Quoth the Raven, "Nevermore."

Much I marvelled this ungainly
Fowl to hear discourse so plainly,
Though its answer little meaning—
Little relevancy bore;
For we cannot help agreeing
That no living human being
Ever yet was blest with seeing
Bird above his chamber door—
Bird or beast upon the sculptured
Bust above his chamber door,
With such name as "Nevermore."

Und trotz meiner Trauer brachte
Er dahin mich, daß ich lachte,
So gesetzt und gravitätisch
    Herrscht' auf meiner Büste er.
„Ob auch alt und nah dem Grabe,"
Sprach ich, „bist kein feiger Knabe,
Schwarzer, glattgeschor'ner Rabe,
    Der Du kamst vom Schattenmeer —
Sprich, welch' stolzen Namen führst Du
    In der Nacht pluton'schem Heer?" —
        Sprach der Rabe: „Nimmermehr."

Ganz erstaunt war ich, zu hören
Dieses Thier mich so belehren,
Schien auch wenig Sinn zu liegen
    In dem Wort bedeutungsleer;
Denn wohl Keiner könnte sagen,
Daß ihm je in seinen Tagen
Sonder Zier und sonder Zagen
    So ein Rab' erschienen wär',
Der auf seiner Marmorbüste
    Ob der Thür gesessen wär'
        Mit dem Namen „Nimmermehr."

But the Raven, sitting lonely
On that placid bust, spoke only
That one word, as if his soul in
That one word he did outpour.
Nothing farther then he uttered;
Not a feather then he fluttered—
Till I scarcely more than muttered,
"Other friends have flown before—
On the morrow *he* will leave me,
As my Hopes have flown before."
Then the bird said, "Nevermore."

Startled at the stillness broken
By reply so aptly spoken,
"Doubtless," said I, "what it utters
Is its only stock and store,
Caught from some unhappy master
Whom unmerciful Disaster
Followed fast and followed faster
Till his songs one burden bore—
Till the dirges of his Hope that
Melancholy burden bore
Of 'Never—nevermore!'"

Dieses Wort nur sprach der Rabe
Dumpf und hohl, wie aus dem Grabe,
Als ob seine ganze Seele
    In dem Einen Worte wär'.
Weiter Nichts ward dann gesprochen,
Nur mein Herz noch hört' ich pochen,
Bis das Schweigen ich gebrochen:
    „Andre Freunde floh'n seither —
Morgen wird auch e r mich fliehen,
    Wie die Hoffnung floh seither."
        Sprach der Rabe: „Nimmermehr."

Immer höher stieg mein Staunen
Bei des Raben dunklem Raunen,
Doch ich dachte: „Ohne Zweifel
    Weiß er weiter sonst Nichts mehr;
Hat's von seinem Herrn gehöret,
Dem das Glück den Rücken kehret,
Dem nur Ungemach bescheeret,
    Bis er trüb und freudenleer —
Bis ihm schwand der Hoffnung Schimmer
    Und er fortan seufzte schwer:
        ‚O nimmer — nimmermehr!'"

But the Raven still beguiling
All my sad soul into smiling,
Straight I wheeled a cushioned seat in
    Front of bird and bust and door;
Then upon the velvet sinking,
I betook myself to linking
Fancy unto fancy, thinking
    What this ominous bird of yore—
What this grim, ungainly, ghastly,
    Gaunt and ominous bird of yore
        Meant in croaking "Nevermore."

This I sat engaged in guessing,
But no syllable expressing
To the fowl whose fiery eyes now
    Burned into my bosom's core;
This and more I sat divining,
With my head at ease reclining
On the cushion's velvet lining
    That the lamplight gloated o'er,
But whose velvet violet lining
    With the lamplight gloating o'er
        She shall press, ah, nevermore!

Der Rabe.

Trotz der Trauer wieder brachte
 Er dahin mich, daß ich lachte;
Einen Armstuhl endlich rollte
 Ich zu Thür und Vogel her.
In den weichen Polstern liegend,
In die Hand die Wange schmiegend,
Sann ich, hin und her mich wiegend,
 Was des Wortes Deutung wär' —
Was der grimme, finstre Vogel
 Aus dem nächt'gen Schattenmeer
 Wollt' mit seinem „Nimmermehr."

Also düster brütend lieg' ich,
 Aber vor dem Vogel schwieg ich,
Dessen Feueraugen jetzo
 Mir das Herz beklemmten sehr;
Dies und mehr bedacht' ich schweigend,
Vorwärts mich und rückwärts beugend,
Dann mich in die Kissen neigend
 Und mich schaukelnd hin und her —
Ach in diesen Sammetkissen,
 Ueberstrahlt vom Lichte hehr,
 Ruhet s i e jetzt nimmermehr!

Then methought the air grew denser,
Perfumed from an unseen censer
Swung by Seraphim whose footfalls
    Tinkled on the tufted floor.
"Wretch," I cried, "thy God hath lent thee—
By these angels he hath sent thee
Respite—respite and nepenthe
    From thy memories of Lenore!
Quaff, oh quaff this kind nepenthe,
    And forget this lost Lenore!"
      Quoth the Raven, "Nevermore."

"Prophet!" said I, "thing of evil!
Prophet still, if bird or devil!—
Whether Tempter sent, or whether
    Tempest tossed thee here ashore,
Desolate, yet all undaunted,
On this desert land enchanted—
On this home by Horror haunted—
    Tell me truly, I implore—
Is there—*is* there balm in Gilead?—
    Tell me—tell me, I implore!"
      Quoth the Raven, "Nevermore."

Und ich wähnte, durch die Lüfte
Zögen süße Weihrauchdüfte,
Ausgestreut durch unsichtbare
  Seraphshände um mich her.
„Gott hat Lethe Dir gespendet
Durch die Engel, die er sendet,
Daß sich Deine Trauer wendet
  Von der Maid, geliebt so sehr!
Nimm, o nimm, was er Dir sendet
  Und vergiß der Trauer schwer!"
   Sprach der Rabe: „Nimmermehr!"

„Gramprophet!" rief ich voll Zweifel,
„Ob Du Vogel oder Teufel! —
Ob die Hölle Dich mir sandte —
  Ob der Sturm Dich wehte her —
Du, der von des Orkus Strande,
Du, der von dem Schreckenslande
Sich zu mir, dem Trüben, wandte —
  Künde mir mein heiß Begehr: —
Find' ich Balsam noch in Gilead? —
  Ist noch Trost im Gnadenmeer?" —
   Sprach der Rabe: „Nimmermehr!"

"Prophet!" said I, "thing of evil!—
Prophet still, if bird or devil!—
By that Heaven that bends above us—
 By that God we both adore—
Tell this soul with sorrow laden
If, within the distant Aidenn,
It shall clasp a sainted maiden
 Whom the angels name Lenore—
Clasp a rare and radiant maiden
 Whom the angels name Lenore."—
  Quoth the Raven, "Nevermore.'

"Be that word our sign of parting,
 Bird or fiend," I shrieked upstarting—
"Get thee back into the tempest
 And the Night's Plutonian shore!
Leave no black plume as a token
Of that lie thy soul hath spoken!
Leave my loneliness unbroken!—
 Quit the bust above my door!
Take thy beak from out my heart, and
 Take thy form from off my door!"
  Quoth the Raven, "Nevermore."

„Gramprophet!" rief ich voll Zweifel,
„Ob Du Vogel oder Teufel! —
Bei dem ew'gen Himmel droben —
    Bei dem Gott, den ich verehr': —
Künde mir, ob ich Lenoren,
Die hienieden ich verloren,
Wieder find' an Edens Thoren,
    Sie, die thront im Himmel hehr —
Jene Sel'ge, die Lenoren
    Nennt der Engel heilig Heer." —
        Sprach der Rabe: „Nimmermehr!"

„Sei dies Wort das Trennungszeichen —
Vogel, Dämon, Du mußt weichen!
Fleuch zurück zum Sturmesgrauen,
    Oder zum pluton'schen Heer!
Keine Feder laß zurücke
Mir als Zeichen deiner Tücke!
Laß allein mich dem Geschicke!
    Wage nie Dich wieder her!
Fort und laß mein Herz in Frieden,
    Das gepeinigt Du so sehr!"
        Sprach der Rabe: „Nimmermehr!"

And the Raven, never flitting,
Still is sitting, still is sitting
On the pallid bust of Pallas
　　Just above my chamber door;
　And his eyes have all the seeming
　Of a demon's that is dreaming,
　And the lamplight o'er him streaming
　　Throws his shadow on the floor;
And my soul from out that shadow,
　　That lies floating on the floor,
　　　　Shall be lifted—NEVERMORE!

Der Rabe.

Und der Rabe weichet nimmer,
Sitzt noch immer, sitzt noch immer
Auf der blassen Pallasbüste
    Ob der Thüre hoch und hehr;
Sitzt mit geisterhaftem Munkeln,
Seine Feueraugen funkeln
Gar dämonisch in dem dunkeln,
    Düstern Schatten um ihn her;
Und mein Geist wird aus dem Schatten,
Den er breitet um mich her,
    Sich erheben — **nimmermehr!**

The Bells.

I.

Hear the sledges with the bells —
　　　Silver bells!
What a world of merriment their melody foretells!
　　How they tinkle, tinkle, tinkle,
　　　In the icy air of night!
　　While the stars that oversprinkle
　　All the heavens, seem to twinkle
　　　With a crystalline delight;
　　Keeping time, time, time,
　　In a sort of Runic rhyme,
To the tintinnabulation that so musically wells
　　From the bells, bells, bells, bells,
　　　Bells, bells, bells —
From the jingling and the tinkling of the bells.

Die Glocken.

I.

Hört die Schlittenglöckchen hell —
        Silberhell!
Welch' unendlich frohe Lust verkündet ihr Geschell!
    Wie sie bimmeln, bimmeln, bimmeln,
    In der eisig kalten Nacht!
    Während an den fernen Himmeln
    Auf und ab die Sterne wimmeln,
        Funkelnd in kryſtall'ner Pracht;
Schwirrend sacht, sacht, sacht,
Bei dem Zaubertakt der Nacht,
Zu dem muſikaliſch ſüßen, freudebringenden Geſchell,
Das so hell, hell, hell, hell,
        Hell, hell, hell —
Zu dem Wimmeln und dem Bimmeln ſilberhell.

II.

Hear the mellow wedding bells—
    Golden bells!
What a world of happiness their harmony foretells!
    Through the balmy air of night
    How they ring out their delight!
      From the molten-golden notes,
        And all in tune,
      What a liquid ditty floats
To the turtle-dove that listens, while she gloats
        On the moon!
    Oh, from out the sounding cells,
What a gush of euphony voluminously wells!
      How it swells!
      How it dwells
    On the Future! how it tells
    Of the rapture that impels
    To the swinging and the ringing
      Of the bells, bells, bells,
    Of the bells, bells, bells, bells,
        Bells, bells, bells—
To the rhyming and the chiming of the bells!

II.

Hört die Hochzeitsglocken hell —
Golden hell!
Welch unendlich süßes Glück verkündet ihr Geschwell!
Durch die Balsamluft der Nacht
Wie es tönt in süßer Pracht!
Welch ein holdes, gold'nes Lied,
Süß betont,
Wonnereich hinüber zieht
Zu der Turteltaube drüben, die da sieht
Nach dem Mond!
Aus des Thurmes enger Zell'
Wie so voll ertönet doch der Glocken süß Geschwell!
Wie so schnell,
Wie so hell
Tönt es, künft'gen Glückes Quell!
Das Entzücken sein Gesell
Bei dem Schwingen und dem Klingen,
Das so hell, hell, hell,
Das so hell, hell, hell, hell,
Hell, hell, hell —
Bei den Sängen und den Klängen, süß und hell!

III.

Hear the loud alarum bells—
Brazen bells!
What a tale of terror, now, their turbulency tells!
In the startled ear of night
How they scream out their affright!
Too much horrified to speak,
They can only shriek, shriek,
Out of tune,
In a clamorous appealing to the mercy of the fire,
In a mad expostulation with the deaf and frantic fire,
Leaping higher, higher, higher,
With a desperate desire,
And a resolute endeavor,
Now—now to sit or never,
By the side of the pale-faced moon.
Oh, the bells, bells, bells!
What a tale their terror tells
Of Despair!
How they clang, and clash, and roar!
What a horror they outpour
On the bosom of the palpitating air!

Die Glocken. 31

III.

Hört die Sturmesglocken grell —
Ehern grell!
Welch ein namenloses Weh verkündet ihr Gegell!
In das bange Ohr der Nacht,
Wie ihr Winseln tönt mit Macht!
Ohne Sang und ohne Klang
Wimmern sie jetzt bang — bang,
Schmerzbetont!
Bald um Gnade wimmernd, winselnd, bei dem unheilvollen Feuer,
Bald sich wuthentbrannt ereifernd mit dem tauben, tollen Feuer,
Das da freier, freier, freier
Aufthürmt sich zum Ungeheuer
Und entschloss'ner strebet immer,
Jetzt zu ruhen, oder nimmer,
Droben bei dem bleichen Mond!
O wie grell, grell, grell,
Doch der Glocken wild Gegell
Jetzo ruft!
Wie es ächzt und krächzt und brüllt!
Wie mit Schauder es erfüllt
Und mit namenlosem Klaggeschrei die Luft!

Yet the ear it fully knows,
By the twanging,
And the clanging,
How the danger ebbs and flows;
Yet the ear distinctly tells,
In the jangling,
And the wrangling,
How the danger sinks and swells,
By the sinking or the swelling in the anger of the bells—
Of the bells—
Of the bells, bells, bells, bells,
Bells, bells, bells—
In the clamor and the clangor of the bells!

IV.

Hear the tolling of the bells—
Iron bells!
What a world of solemn thought their monody compels!
In the silence of the night,
How we shiver with affright
At the melancholy menace of their tone!

Doch erräth das Ohr es leicht,
Bei dem Gellen
Und dem Bellen,
Wie das Feuer fällt und steigt;
Dennoch merkt das Ohr es schnell,
Bei dem Dröhnen
Und dem Stöhnen,
Ob es sinke oder schwell';
Bei dem Sinken oder Schwellen in der Glocken Sturmgebell,
Das so grell —
Das so grell, grell, grell, grell,
Grell, grell, grell —
Bei dem Aechzen und dem Krächzen wild und grell!

IV.

Hört die Todtenglocken grell —
Eisern grell!
O wie ernst und feierlich ertönet ihr Geschwell!
In dem Schweigen dunkler Nacht
Welch ein Schaudern doch erwacht
Bei der Glocken melancholischem Gedröhn!

For every sound that floats
From the rust within their throats
  Is a groan.
And the people—ah, the people—
They that dwell up in the steeple,
  All alone,
And who, tolling, tolling, tolling,
  In that muffled monotone,
Feel a glory in so rolling
  On the human heart a stone—
They are neither man nor woman—
They are neither brute nor human—
  They are Ghouls:
  And their king it is who tolls;
  And he rolls, rolls, rolls,
   Rolls
  A pæan from the bells!
And his merry bosom swells
  With the pæan of the bells!
And he dances, and he yells;
Keeping time, time, time,
In a sort of Runic rhyme,
  To the pæan of the bells—
   Of the bells:

Die Glocken.

Denn jeder Ton, der fließt
Aus dem ehernen Schlunde, ist
    Ein Gestöhn.
Und die Leute, die da hausen
Auf dem Thurme sonder Grausen,
    Ganz allein,
Die mit Grollen, Grollen, Grollen
    Laben sich an unf'rer Pein,
Die es freut, hinabzurollen
    Auf die Herzen Stein um Stein —
Es sind keine Erdgestalten,
Es sind Geister, die da walten
    Nimmer hold:
Und ihr König ist's, der grollt,
Und er rollt, rollt, rollt,
    Rollt
    Ein Grablied grimm und grell!
Und sein Busen hebt sich schnell
    Bei dem Grablied grimm und grell!
Und er tanzt von Stell' zu Stell'
Schwirrend sacht, sacht, sacht,
Bei dem Zaubertakt der Nacht,
    Zu dem Grablied grimm und grell —
    Grimm und grell:

Keeping time, time, time,
In a sort of Runic rhyme,
    To the throbbing of the bells—
Of the bells, bells, bells—
    To the sobbing of the bells;
Keeping time, time, time,
    As he knells, knells, knells,
In a happy Runic rhyme,
    To the rolling of the bells—
Of the bells, bells, bells—
    To the tolling of the bells,
Of the bells, bells, bells, bells,
    Bells, bells, bells—
To the moaning and the groaning of the bells!

Die Glocken.

Schwirrend sacht, sacht, sacht,
Bei dem Dämontakt der Nacht,
   Zu der Glocken Grabgegell;
Das so grell, grell, grell —
   Zu der Glocken Grabgeschwell;
Schwirrend sacht, sacht, sacht,
   In der Zell', Zell', Zell',
Bei dem Geistertakt der Nacht,
   Zu dem rollenden Gegell —
Das so grell, grell, grell,
   Zu dem grollenden Gegell —
Das so grell, grell, grell, grell,
   Grell, grell, grell —
Zu dem Dröhnen und dem Stöhnen, grimm und grell!

Lenore.

I.

Ah, broken is the golden bowl!
    The spirit flown forever!
Let the bell toll! — a saintly soul
    Floats on the Stygian river!
And, Guy de Vere, hast *thou* no tear?
    Weep now or nevermore!
See! on yon drear and rigid bier
    Low lies thy love, Lenore!
Come! Let the burial-rite be read —
    The funeral song be sung!—
An anthem for the queenliest dead
    That ever died so young —
A dirge for her, the doubly dead,
    In that she died so young!

Lenore.

I.

Zerbrochen ist der gold'ne Halt
    Gelöst des Geistes Bann!
Ihr Glocken schallt! — die Sel'ge wallt
    Den dunkeln Styr hinan!
Und Guy de Vere, weinst Du nicht hier? —
    Wein' jetzt, wenn nie zuvor!
Denn sieh' vor Dir, so starr und stier,
    Liegt Deine Lieb', Lenor'! —
Singt nach des Rituals Gebot
    Ein Anthem nun im Schwung
Für sie, die Herrlichste — nun todt —
    Die jemals starb so jung —
Ein Lied für sie, die doppelt todt,
    Dieweil sie starb so jung!

II.

"Wretches, ye loved her for her wealth,
    And hated her for her pride,
And when she fell in feeble health,
    Ye blessed her — that she died!
How *shall* the ritual, then, be read ?—
    The requiem how be sung ?
By you — by yours, the evil eye, —
    By yours, the slanderous tongue,
That did to death the innocence
    That died, and died so young ?"

III.

Peccavimus; but rave not thus!
    And let a Sabbath song
Go up to God so solemnly
    The dead may feel no wrong!
The sweet Lenore hath "gone before,"
    With Hope that flew beside,
Leaving thee wild for the dear child
    That should have been thy bride —

II.

„Heuchler, ihr liebtet nur ihr Gut
  Und haßtet ihr Gemüth,
Und als versiegt die Lebensflut,
  Da freut' euch's — daß sie schied!
Wer, nach des Rituals Gebot,
  Singt's Requiem nun im Schwung?
Ihr — ihr, verruchte Lästerer,
  Die ihr mit falscher Zung'
Zu Tod gequält die Heilige,
  Die starb, und starb so jung?"

III.

Peccavimus; doch raf' nicht so!
  Laß einen Sabbathsang
Zum Himmel steigen sacht empor
  Mit feierlichem Klang!
Denn ach, Lenor' — sie ging zuvor,
  Die Hoffnung folgt' vertraut
Und ließ Dich wild und schmerzerfüllt
  Um Deine todte Braut —

For her, the fair and *debonair*,
    That now so lowly lies,
The life upon her yellow hair,
    But not within her eyes —
The life still there upon her hair —
    The death upon her eyes.

IV.

"Avaunt! to-night my heart is light!
    No dirge will I upraise,
But waft the angel on her flight
    With a Pæan of old days!
Let *no* bell toll! — lest her sweet soul,
    Amid its hallowed mirth,
Should catch the note, as it doth float
    Up from the damnéd Earth.
To friends above, from fiends below,
    The indignant ghost is riven —
From Hell unto a high estate
    Far up within the Heaven —
From grief and groan to a golden throne
    Beside the King of Heaven!"

Die immerdar so lieblich war,
    Und todt nun — o Geschick!
Des Lebens Hauch im gold'nen Haar,
    Doch nicht in ihrem Blick —
Das Leben klar noch auf dem Haar —
    Doch Tod in ihrem Blick!

IV.

"Hinfort! entweicht! Mein Herz ist leicht!
    Nicht will ich klagen heut;
Ich weih' dem Engel, der da fleucht,
    Päane früh'rer Zeit!
Kein Glockenschall! daß nicht ihr Hall
    An ihre Ohren gellt,
Dieweil empor zu Edens Thor
    Sie flieht von arger Welt;
Zu Freunden dort, von Feinden hier,
    Seh' ihren Geist ich schweben —
Von Höllenqual zum lichten Thal,
    Fern, fern, im schönern Leben —
Von Haß und Hohn zum gold'nen Thron,
    Den Gott ihr dort wird geben!"

The Rose.

I.

In his tower sat the poet
  Gazing on the roaring sea,
"Take this rose," he sighed, "and throw it
  Where there's none that loveth me!
On the rock the billow bursteth
  And sinks back into the seas,
But in vain my spirit thirsteth
  So to burst and be at ease.
Take, o sea! the tender blossom
  That hath lain against my breast;
On thy black and angry bosom
  It will find a surer rest.
Life is vain, and love is hollow,
  Ugly death stands there behind,

Die Rose.

I.

Auf dem Thurme sitzt der Dichter,
    Schaut auf's Meer, vom Sturm bewegt;
„Bring die Rose hin," so spricht er,
    „Wo kein liebend Herz mir schlägt.
An den Fels die Welle dröhnet,
    Fällt dann in die Flut zurück;
Doch umsonst mein Herz sich sehnet,
    So zu finden Ruh' und Glück.
Nimm, o See! die zarten Blüten,
    Die an meiner Brust geruht;
Sichre Rast und tiefern Frieden
    Finden sie in deiner Flut.
Hohl ist Lieb' und Lust auf Erden,
    Grimmen Tod die Zukunft birgt;

Hate and scorn and hunger follow
    Him that toileth for his kind."
Forth into the night he hurled it,
    And with bitter smile did mark
How the surly tempest whirled it
    Swift into the hungry dark.
Foam and spray drive back to leeward,
    And the gale with dreary moan,
Drifts the helpless blossom seaward,
    Through the breakers all alone.

II.

Stands a maiden, on the morrow,
    Musing by the wave-beat strand,
Half in hope and half in sorrow,
    Tracing words upon the sand:
"Shall I ever then behold him
    Who hath been my life so long, —
Ever to this sick heart fold him, —
    Be the spirit of his song?
Touch not, sea, the blessed letters
    I have traced upon thy shore

Haß und Hohn und Hunger werden
　　Dem, der für die Menschheit wirkt."
In die Nacht warf er die Rose,
　　Bitter lächelnd schaute er,
Wie der Wogen wild Getose
　　Warf sie wirbelnd hin und her.
Gischt und Brandung tobten leewärts
　　Und des rauhen Windes Macht
Trieb das zarte Blümchen seewärts,
　　Hilflos durch die dunkle Nacht.

II.

Steht die Jungfrau drauf am Morgen
　　Sinnend an des Meeres Strand;
Halb in Hoffnung, halb in Sorgen —
　　Schreibt sie Worte in den Sand:
„Werd' ich ihn denn je erblicken,
　　Der mein Herz erfüllt so lang?
Je an diese Brust ihn drücken —
　　Leben je in seinem Sang?
Laß, o See! den theuren Namen,
　　Den ich schrieb auf deinen Strand —

Spare his name whose spirit fetters
    Mine with love forevermore!"
Swells the tide and overflows it,
    But, with omen pure and meet,
Brings a little rose, and throws it
    Humbly at the maiden's feet.
Full of bliss she takes the token,
    And, upon her snowy breast,
Soothes the ruffled petals broken
    With the ocean's fierce unrest.
"Love is thine, o heart! and surely
    Peace shall also be thine own,
For the heart that trusteth purely
    Never long can pine alone."

III.

In his tower sits the poet,
    Blisses new and strange to him
Fill his heart and overflow it
    With a wonder sweet and dim.
Up the beach the ocean slideth
    With a whisper of delight,

Schon' der Worte, die da kamen
  Aus dem Herzen liebentbrannt!"
Schwillt der Schwall und wischt die Worte
  Weg — doch, wie ein ferner Gruß,
Ruht ein Röschen an dem Orte
  Zitternd vor der Jungfrau Fuß.
Freuderfüllt nahm sie die Rose,
  Schmiegt an ihre Schwanenbrust
Sie mit liebendem Gekose
  Und mit nimmersatter Lust.
„Herz! der Liebe Thor ist offen,
  Friede auch wird sicher dein;
Denn der Seele treues Hoffen
  Schmachtet nimmer lang allein."

III.

Auf dem Thurme sitzt der Dichter,
  Neue, nie geahnte Lust
Füllt sein Herz, der Hoffnung Lichter
  Leuchten hell in seiner Brust.
Fern hinaus das Meer sich breitet
  Wispernd, wonnig, weich und sacht,

THE ROSE.

And the moon in silence glideth
    Through the peaceful blue of night.
Rippling o'er the poet's shoulder
    Flows a maiden's golden hair,
Maiden-lips, with love grown bolder,
    Kiss his moon-lit forehead bare.
"Life is joy, and love is power,
    Death all fetters doth unbind,
Strength and wisdom only flower
    When we toil for all our kind.
Hope is truth, — the future giveth
    More than present takes away,
And the soul forever liveth
    Nearer God from day to day."
Not a word the maiden uttered,
    Fullest hearts are slow to speak,
But a withered rose-leaf fluttered
    Down upon the poet's cheek.

Die Rose.

Und des Mondes Kugel gleitet
    Durch das tiefe Blau der Nacht.
Um des Dichters Brust und Arme
    Wallt der Jungfrau golden Haar;
Mädchenlippen, liebewarme,
    Küssen seine Stirne klar.
„Lieb' und Lust durch's Leben glühen,
    Selbst der Tod nur Freiheit bringt;
Kraft und Weisheit Dem nur blühen,
    Der für's Wohl der Menschheit ringt.
Hoffnung siegt — die Zukunft schenket
    Mehr noch als das Jetzt uns raubt;
Näher stets zur Gottheit lenket
    Sich das Herz, das innig glaubt."
Stumm hält ihn die Maid umfangen,
    Denn des Herzens Fülle schweigt —
Aber auf des Dichters Wangen
    Sich ein welkes Röschen neigt.

STEIN & JONES, Printers,
521 Chestnut Street, Philadelphia.